A ROOKIE READER®

LARRY AND THE COOKIE

By Becky Bring McDaniel

Illustrated by Clovis Martin

Prepared under the direction of Robert Hillerich, Ph.D.

CHILDRENS PRESS®
CHICAGO

In loving memory
of Barbara Kirkpatrick

Library of Congress Cataloging-in-Publication Data

McDaniel, Becky Bring.
    Larry and the cookie / by Becky Bring McDaniel ;
illustrated by Clovis Martin.
        p.   cm. — (A Rookie reader)
    Summary: After playing on the slide and swing,
riding his bike, and playing basketball and football,
Larry has trouble finding the cookie he stashed in his
pocket.
    ISBN 0-516-02014-5
    [1. Cookies—Fiction. 2. Play—Fiction.] I. Martin,
Clovis, ill. II. Title. III. Series.
PZ7.M13995Lar   1993
[E]—dc20   92-37871
                                CIP
                                AC

Larry found one cookie in the cookie jar.
It was his favorite kind.

He put it
in his pocket
for later.

4

Then he went outside to play.

Larry played on the swing.

He checked the cookie;
it was still there.

Larry played on the slide.

12

He checked the cookie;
it was still there.

Larry rode his bike.

15

He checked the cookie;
it was still there.

Larry played basketball.

He checked the cookie;
it was still there.

21

22

Larry played football.

He checked the cookie;
but it was gone!

Larry looked for his cookie.
He looked up and down.

He looked all around.
But the cookie could
not be found.

Larry checked his pocket
one more time.
He reached way down
and felt something.

Out came his hand full of crumbs.
Larry had found his cookie!

WORD LIST

			of	something
all	crumbs	he	on	still
and	down	his	one	swing
around	favorite	in	out	the
basketball	felt	it	outside	then
be	football	jar	play	there
bike	for	kind	played	time
but	found	Larry	pocket	to
came	full	later	put	up
checked	gone	looked	reached	was
cookie	had	more	rode	way
could	hand	not	slide	went

About the Author

Becky Bring McDaniel was born in Ashland, Ohio, but spent approximately half her life in Gainesville, Florida, where she is pursuing a degree in creative writing at the University of Florida. Several of her poems have been published in such magazines as *Creative Years, The National Girl Scout Magazine,* and *Writers' Opportunities.* She is married and has three children. She has several other manuscripts in progress and looks forward to a career in writing for children.

About the Artist

Clovis Martin has enjoyed a varied career as an art director, designer, and illustrator of children's books and other educational products. Two books illustrated by Mr. Martin were selected for the prestigious "Children's Choices" list, a project of the IRA/Children's Book Council. He lives with his wife, two daughters, and his son in Cleveland Heights, Ohio.